MW00936895

Once Upon A Star

Michelle Novak

Delilah,
Enjoy the magic!
Best Wishes,
Michelle

For Ruslana

Chapter One

Lomina was on a journey. She and her elder sister Cora were sitting upon embroidered cushions in the back of an open wagon. Their transport was being pulled by two beautiful brown mares, with glossy coats and brushed manes. Their brother Ackerly, the eldest of the siblings, held the reins that drove them. So far, the trip had been long and uncomfortable, as travel usually was.

Their parents, Lord and Lady Umberly, rode upon fine horses covered with polished leather saddles. If Lomina (who was called Mina for short) and Cora had been more practiced, the entire family would have rode on horseback. They would have galloped past villages and through fields at a much faster pace, leaving a trusted steward to manage their wagon. But the girls had not taken enough riding lessons for them to make the journey safely upon a horse.

The cart was also carrying the family's trunks, filled with their clothes and belongings. There was some furniture too, which sometimes bumped into the girls when the wagon drove over a branch or rock in the road. It was late summer and hot. During the hottest hours at midday, attendants mounted a small canopy over the wagon to shade the girls from the sun. But Mina and Cora preferred to see all of the places that they were passing as they went, even if it was hot and the creaky wooden wheels stirred up dust, which got in their eyes and noses.

Mina would miss their home very much, and had never traveled so far before. There had been a few trips to local hamlets to see an ancient church or to shop for goods in a busy market, but this was very different indeed. Her parents had not been born nobles, but her father had greatly pleased the king with his excellent service, who then bestowed special titles and favors upon their family. Lord and Lady Umberly had been enjoying such privileges since even before any of their children had been born. What had Mina's father done to be rewarded high status in the realm, and to receive a good life of comfort from a king? Toly Umberly was good at solving problems. Not political problems, where people fought over lands and power. His talents were quite different.

Toly had lost his farming parents as a boy to a terrible sickness that had spread through the land. As an orphan, he was taken in by the local and learned monks, who sometimes taught rich noble sons their lessons, for a fee. From the monks, Toly learned a great many things, like how to grow plants, masonry to build strong structures and also how to care for animals. He worked hard to complete the chores that they gave him, which kept a roof over his head and hearty food in his stomach.

They also taught him to read and write, even though he was not a noble boy.

Though books were rare and expensive, the monks did keep a small library filled with ancient texts. One kind monk frequently sent Toly to the library to dust it, knowing that the boy would disappear for several hours, reading those old volumes. Toly had several favorites that he often looked through, turning their fragile parchment pages with care. They were books about the enchanted beings and wild creatures that lived throughout the world. These were not the common denizens found in the forests and fields.

There were the mermen and mermaids that lived in the seas, who had no legs, but rather the tails of fish. There were even different types, such as the kind of mermen called blue men. These mermen had blue skin and upon their faces, they grew thick ashen beards. The blue men were said to be very unruly and had powers over the waves and weather, causing squalls and storms to shipwreck hapless sailors. If you were sailing at sea with your crew and you encountered a blue man, there was only one hope for escape, an excellent riddle too hard for a blue man to solve. Before stirring up the elements, a blue man would allow the captain of the ship to give him a riddle. If it were too easy, the men would be in peril. If the blue man could not figure it out, he'd let the ship pass through the waters unharmed. Toly thought that every seaman should keep a clever riddle in his memory before stepping one toe off land!

There were griffins, enormous flying beasts that lived on the craggy peaks of mountains. They had powerful beaks, sharp claws and impressive wings, just like a predatory bird. But their bodies were muscular and furry, much like a cat's. Those who had seen one said it looked like an eagle and a lion were one. Griffins stole gold from humans, swooping in and clawing at their shiny necklaces, ripping the gilded ornaments from off of noble castles, and snatching up aurous emblems anywhere they could find them. Griffins loved gold so much that they layered the metal amongst the branches that made their nests. They also devoured horses, their favorite meal. If Toly lived near a mountain, and were rich enough to own gold, he would certainly never flaunt it outside of his house!

Then there were the giants, which lived in almost every realm, but were reclusive. Though many believed that they were the size of a house, it was not true. Giants were very large indeed, but only about three times the size of any normal man. They did not live in cottages, or take baths, or cook their meals. They were wild, abiding in caves, stinky and dirty, eating whatever they could find and leaving it raw. Though they kept to themselves, occasionally an evil ruler would lure them into his battles, to use their brute strength to fight against his foes. He'd pay the giants with stores of poor food and treat them unkindly. Toly thought that people should leave the giants alone and never take advantage of them, for they were citizens of the realm, just as any person was. It wasn't right for them to be mistreated, or to place them in danger.

There were dwarves too, who were a little like the Griffins in loving gold. What they cared for most in the world, were the minerals found deep below the ground and the metals that came from out of the earth. They understood more than men, how important it was to leave these materials alone to sleep, and found clever ways to protect the earth by stopping humans from mining it all until there was nothing left. They believed that using a little was ok; a bit of metal for a horseshoe or some silver for spoon. But to mine tons of earth to grow rich upon made dwarves sad, and angry too. Greedy kings and disgruntled dwarves had fought for this very reason, in ancient times. Toly understood why the dwarves protected the earth. He'd once seen a beloved forest filled with wise old trees, razed to the ground for wood to build a village and was heartbroken to see those woods destroyed.

Living with the monks, Toly learned more and more from the books, and took lessons from the wisest of these men. He worked hard to help keep their humble church and dwellings in good repair, to thank them for teaching him many new topics as he grew. By the time Toly Umberly was a young man, he was quite educated for the son of a farmer and was granted a good position as a chancellor to a noble lord with a manor house close to the king's castle. Chancellors wrote letters, organized confidential papers, cared for precious documents and books and gave good advice on urgent matters.

Before he knew it, Toly was accompanying his noble employer to the castle, to scribble notes during important courtly meetings. This was very exciting, for Toly was learning so many things about the realm, by listening in on discussions amongst the peerage. The members of the king's noble court were dazzling in their rich garments, and the castle was magnificent. The meals he'd enjoyed there had been the most delicious he'd ever eaten. But what Toly loved the best, was the castle library! Of the mounds of books piled upon tables and the walls stuffed with dusty volumes, what great things he could learn! Alas, he had no right to linger in that part of the castle and could only look longingly on the room, each time he passed it.

And then one day, the most incredible thing happened. After some years as a chancellor, working hard for the noble he served, he was summoned before the king. King Olin had taken notice of Toly's intelligence and thoughtful input when it was sometimes required during court discussions. The king wanted to know more about this Toly Umberly. Where was he from, and how had he received such a good education? What were his interests and skills? Kings were always looking for smart people to serve the realm.

As it turned out, Toly had knowledge that King Olin would find useful. The young man knew more about the wild and enchanted beings and animals of the land, than anyone the king had ever met before. The king had long had to deal with difficult situations that arose between his citizens and that world of mystery and magic. The king could use a good man like Toly to bring any skirmishes to a quick end, intelligently and with care. The man for the position would be appointed knights to aid him in his work, and fine titles and rewards if he could keep the kingdom at peace concerning these matters. And of course, he would be able to make as much use of the castle library as he wished. Toly knelt before the king, and accepted this most enormous, and most adventurous task.

Chapter Two

As Lomina bumped along in the wagon, she thought about all of the valorous missions her father had been on. When he was at home, with his wife and children, Lord Umberly told a great many tales around the hearth, of all the amazing creatures that lived throughout the land, and about the many conflicts that he'd helped lay to rest.

The funniest of the stories was about a large village with an odd problem. Next to this town, a vast woodland grew, which was dense and wild. The village was a peaceful one and crime was rarely heard of. But then one day, a few things went missing. Some wool yarn here, a shiny coin there, a wax candle here, a bone sewing needle there. The citizens of the town simply thought they'd lost these things, for there was nothing much missing and their houses didn't appear to have been broken into.

Soon however, the wives of the village

began to complain to one another as they washed their laundry in the stream, of what had gone astray. It soon seemed clear that *a lot* of folks were missing things, and the problem was only getting worse! Before they knew it, buttons were removed from shirts and shoes, children's dolls and little wooden toys vanished, dishes made of pewter were taken and any precious trinkets in sight were snatched up. Yet the people of this village were baffled, for their cottages were small and they had been unable to catch any human thieves going in or out of their houses. Even travelers passing through the town, stopping at the village inn to rest a while and eat a meal, would return to their horses and wagons, only to find things amiss: a traveling trunk open and items scattered, or bits of wood, leather and shiny fixtures from their transport torn away. Often costly things were left behind, while things of lesser value (however useful to the villagers and travelers) were taken. It was quite the mystery!

One summer's afternoon, the blacksmith's wife had gone out with her basket to collect wild raspberries at the edge of the woods, leaving the wooden shutters of her little house wide open so that a breeze might run through her home and cool things off. She didn't get far from her dwelling however, before a fierce wind blew up and the sunny day began to grow cloudy with the skies starting to rumble. A thunderstorm was coming. Hurrying back to her house, she was met with an unexpected scene! As she entered her cottage, all was dark. The wind had smacked her window shutters closed, and without a fire lit within, she could hardly see.

As she stumbled toward a window to let in some light and start some candles before the storm set in, she heard a noise. It sounded as though something had fallen from the table onto the floor. And then there was another noise, was it the clanking of cups? A twig snapped from where the woodpile should be. What were these sounds, thought the blacksmith's wife, for she had no cat and only rarely did a mouse scurry through her house. As she inched along, getting closer to the window, little rustling noises here and there could be heard around the room. Had some birds come down her chimney? What if it were bats? She didn't like bats!

With her hands stretched out before her in the darkness, something small skimmed against her arm, and the slightest whoosh of air could be felt. Fearing that it was indeed a bat, she screeched! All at once, what sounded like a dozen tiny screeches rang out after hers and the commotion in the room increased tenfold. It sounded as though creatures were bumping into walls, knocking things over, and making quite a mess. Whatever animals had gotten into her cottage, they hadn't only frightened her, but it sounded as though she had given them quite a scare as well! Hurrying to the window, she threw open her shutters and the light from outside flooded in.

Fairies! A band of naughty, thieving, mess making, intruders! A cloud of creatures from the world of faes, enchanted and wild! The blacksmith's wife could hardly believe her eyes as they flitted around the room, zooming past her nose as they tried to find their way out of her house. They seemed truly frightened of her. She was afraid too, for what if one of them bit her finger or pinched her cheek. She'd heard that they were fierce little biters and pinchers. How awful! But worse still, they were magical and might play a horrible trick on her for scaring them so. What if one of them blew into both her ears and made them turn into fuzzy cat ears? Or what if one danced upon her head and made her hair turn colors?

It was said that such magic tricks wore off in a day or two, but how frightening!

The fairies were dazzling (but that didn't stop her from screeching and screeching until her neighbors came running). They flitted through the room like silent hummingbirds; their iridescent wings could hardly be seen as they skimmed through the air. They wore miniature clothes and adornments right from nature: leaves, feathers, moss, flower petals. Each glowed ever so slightly in the prettiest colors to be seen! Pink, yellow, blue and green. Was this an effect of their current excitement? They were zipping around the room so fast, that closer details were impossible to see. Were those pointy ears that she saw?

One by one, the creatures flew out of the open window. Not a single one was left behind to question about this intrusion. Though, even if there had been, it was unlikely that they spoke the same language as humans!

However, it was very clear from the general disarray of the cottage that the village thief had been no person at all, but a horde of fairies! This could not be stood for, or the townspeople would have nothing left to own. What could be done?

King Olin was plied, and Lord Umberly and his men sent to the town. After they roamed the nearby forest (where it was certain the fairies lived), a great many stolen items were discovered. Shiny objects hanging in trees, little baubles stacked upon rocks, laces and strings wound around a great many branches. The fairies were decorating their woodland realm with their special finds.

This was tricky, for the fairies had surely meant no harm by filching the trifles that they found so wondrous. Further, any being of the realm of faes could be easily agitated. If they tried to punish the fairies, it would anger them. They might begin playing far more naughty tricks. But Toly had a plan.

All of the villagers were instructed to gather their useless rubbish, a broken this or a well-worn that. A handful of pieces a day were to be left on one enormous flat stone aside the enchanted wood. On that first day, far less disturbances were noted in the village, and the offerings were found to be all gone from the stone. And as the days drew on, travelers passing through heard of this experiment to save the village from fairy plunder, and also began leaving their wasted trinkets and bits. It not only amused the wayfarers to do so, but they also hoped that the act would protect their horses and wagons from being picked at as they dined at the inn. Before long, the fairies seemed so satisfied with the items left on their rock, that they looted the villagers of their most useful possessions no more. Umberly's strategy had worked, at least for now.

Lomina's father had solved a great many

such problems, in a great many villages. There were grumpy dragons to calm, and monstrous birds to placate. There were wise elves to reason with and blue men of the sea to riddle. Usually, it was easy to see why humans and enchanted creatures were at odds. They just didn't understand one another. It had been very rare however that something could not be sorted out and quickly too, once Lord Umberly gave his expert council (except that one time when that enormous one-eyed ogre just *would not stop* dragging off those villagers' milking cows to eat for his supper).

Looking out over the lush green fields, with the glorious sun beating down on her bare head (which was coiled atop with pretty braids), Mina wondered how her father would manage his next missions. The whole family was heading to what felt like the edge of the earth, where the skies were said to glow pink at dusk and dawn, signaling the hour when enchanted creatures loved most to come out and play. Their new home would be Castle Eerie, one of the most mysterious dwellings in the realm. It was a place filled with hidden pathways secreted behind stone walls, a castle said to shelter a hobgoblin in every room (behind the embroidered wall hangings and inside aged storage trunks). Who knew what citizens of the enchanted realm they were to meet around this castle. Mina would have to be courageous, especially as she walked through the halls of the castle by candlelight at night; or so said her sister Cora with a giggle.

Chapter Three

When they reached the castle, it was long after dark and Lomina and Cora were fast asleep in the wagon. They both woke suddenly, sleepy and confused by the sounds of rustling and of hurried voices. They'd arrived at the castle and fretful grooms and menservants were working to take their horses to the stable and sort out their trunks. It was very dark, except for several flaming torches lighting one archaic and stony archway. The entryway looked creepy to Mina, who was remembering her sister's words about needing to be brave in this place.

After the family gathered from off of their mounts and the wagon, she clung close-by to her parents as they went through the passageway, led by attendants with torches. They trailed within an echoing hall of carved rock, soon exiting out into a large open courtyard. Lomina could feel the puzzled together, roughly cut stones underfoot and wondered how long ago they'd been set in place. A bright round moon glowed overhead. Up around the square, the walls of Castle Eerie rose out of the darkness and she could see several lit windows high above.

Soon, they entered through a massive wooden door and were met with a warm light. There was to be found inside, a long hall filled with candles upon side tables, the walls dotted with candled sconces. There were lamps aglow with candlelight as well, festooned from high above from the ceiling. Everywhere was stone, the floor, ceiling and walls. What a formidable fortress!

Lomina was very tired and could hardly lift her feet, tripping along the way as she and her family were led down the long hall, also filled with carved wooden furniture, paintings and wall hangings. The embroidered wall coverings looked to be filled with stories, every stitch helping to retell some ancient tale. One day soon, she'd slowly walk past each one and try to figure out what adventures, romances and tragedies they told. She'd ask Cora to come along and help her decipher them.

The family weaved past rooms with blazing fireplaces, the flames illuminating the chambers to look like secret caverns. There would be so many unique places to explore here! One room was covered wall-to-wall with shelves supporting dusty manuscripts and old scrolls rolled into weathered leather. There were tables and chairs too, so that one could sit and read. They also passed a grand meeting hall, with long tables and benches stretching down either side of the room. That would certainly be the place they'd take their meals. Lomina imagined it full of people for an evening of feasting. There would be delicious roasted foods and sweet treats, music and dancing too. She loved special days of the year, when neighbors gathered for a merry celebration.

In another room, numerous windows lined the walls amidst the thick stone. There were wooden stools and stands aplenty. Several of the stands captured and pulled taut squares of fabric, displaying new embroidered pieces that were being worked on. The light that would flood into that room during the day was excellent for those who stitched; embroidery was painstaking work and hard on the eyes. Mina wondered how many of the wall hangings around the castle had been made in that room over the centuries.

They also passed an enormous kitchen, outfitted with *three* fireplaces, each as big as a dragon's belly! Before one, several bulbous black kettles hung over hot coals upon the flat stones just outside of the fire. She wondered what was cooking in them this evening. Boiling potatoes in one and a hearty barley stew in the other perhaps. With a castle as large as this one, and acres of grounds as well, the estate needed a great many people to run it. Therefore, there would be many mouths to feed. The fires likely stood burning at every hour of day and night, in winter and in summer. Mina thought that her father must be very important to the king, since their family had been chosen to live here. This was an honor not many nobles would have been bestowed.

Lady Umberly and the girls came to a sudden stop in the castle as several maidservants approached. Lord Umberly and Ackerly continued on, soon veering off down separate halls, each being guided to their individual rooms. Their mother kissed each of them on the forehead and told them both to have sweet dreams.

"And if you are lucky, grassland fairies from the fields around the castle will sneak in through the cracks of your shuttered windows as you sleep." Lady Umberly said to them with a wink.

Mina gasped, so very tired but with her eyes widened by her mother's remark. "But mother! They might pinch our toes as we doze!"

"Ah, no! For grassland fairies come to do but one thing in the night. Dance on your head!" The elegant lady smiled and patted Cora's pretty plaits.

"Oh, don't tease! What would they do *that* for?" Cora looked anxious.

Their mother bent down and whispered to them both as the maidservants waited patiently nearby. "They twirl and prance on your head when you sleep, to give you the most wonderful dreams there are to be had. It is a kindness."

"Mother, is that true?" Mina peeped.

"Yes, it is. And after a night of such

pleasant imaginings, you'll wake to find a telltale sign of their visit." Lady Umberly arched one eyebrow mysteriously.

"Oh! *What*?" Cora whispered loudly, "What is this sign?"

The woman stood upright and pulled both of them to her, hugging them tightly. "You will know when it happens. I'll let this be a surprise. Now, I bid you not to be afraid of *any* enchanted creature in this realm, and especially not a little grassland fairy or wood sprite. Your father has worked hard to keep peace between their world and ours. You girls are both his children, smart and brave like he, and your brother Ackerly too. If you meet a magical creature during our time at Castle Eerie, be you kind and thoughtful. No shrieking. Do you understand?"

The girls nodded in unison, but then Cora gasped and pulled away. "But *what if* it is a dragon, or an ogre?"

"Run for home as fast as you can. Little girls should have no dealings with those beasts. However, they can't help their temperaments and should not be despised. They are still a part of our world and deserve our respect. Just stay clear. Now off to bed!" Lady Umberly softly pushed them toward the maidservants, one for each to lead them to their very own bedchambers.

Chapter Four

Lomina was uncertain about sleeping in her very own room. Usually, she shared a chamber with her sister, and they would laugh and tell stories before falling asleep each night. She might feel alone, even frightened, in a room all to herself in this new place. But then, the handmaiden showed her into one of the finest chambers and she was instantly overwhelmed with excitement! The place was aglow with the light of a warming fireplace. To one side of the room, an enormous four-poster bed stood, with a fabric canopy over its top and curtains pulled back that could be drawn around it. The bed itself was covered in a downy coverlet. Who needed fairies to prance on one's head if you had a luxurious bed like *that*? Mina would already be having a good rest and pleasant dreams aplenty, in such a comfortable nest! She was so sleepy, she couldn't wait to crawl in.

A male attendant entered the room and sat one of Lomina's trunks on the floor, right next to a lofty free-standing wooden closet, and then walked out again, shutting the door behind him. The maid promptly opened it and riffled through until she found what she was looking for, one of Mina's bed gowns. She laid it upon the bed and then went about fluffing the blankets and the feather stuffed bolster.

Lomina looked around curiously. There were several shuttered windows, drawn tightly. She didn't think a fairy could slip through. There was a small table set with two chairs near the fireplace, several storage trunks and a bedside table with wooden legs carved to look like weaving vines. There was a ceramic washbasin painted with pretty blue cornflowers around its rim, propped up on a wood stand. There were also velvety fabric hangings covering most of the stone walls. Those thick folds surely kept cold drafts at bay on wintery days and nights. Upon the table before the fire, a pewter vase displayed a fresh bouquet of pink roses. When she wasn't so tired, she'd plant her face in them and smell those pretty buds.

How lucky she was! With as cozy and inviting as the room was, she wouldn't be afraid to sleep alone at all. She felt as though the chamber had been perfectly chosen, just for her!

"Are you hungry mistress? Should I bring you a hot bowl of soup or a cup of warmed milk before you go to sleep?" Inquired the handmaiden with a kind smile.

"Oh, no. For I am so tired. I just wish to go to sleep if I may, but I thank you. Oh, what is your name? I'm so sleepy I almost forgot my manners! I am Lomina, but everyone calls me Mina." She shared politely.

"How nice to meet you Mistress Lomina. I am Grace. I am sure that you are quite worn out, for you have traveled from very far. Well now, I'll come to look in on you in the morning." The handmaiden told her.

"But wait...is it true what they say? That the lands around Castle Eerie glow with pink illumination at dawn and dusk? And, that enchanted creatures are more likely to be seen at those hours?" She asked with wonder showing on her face.

Grace chuckled, "Why yes! It *is* true! They say it is because there is so much magic in this exact part of the realm, that it changes the light! But no more questions this night, for it is nearly morning and you need your sleep." She laughed lightly once more. "As curious as *you* are, you'll want to do some exploring tomorrow, I have no doubt!"

The handmaiden appeared to be in her early twenties, plainly dressed but her clothes clean, and crisp from an iron. A thick brown braid was plaited into a bun at the back of her head and her face was ruddy from hard work, and the good health of her youth. She seemed very nice and Lomina was pleased to know someone at the castle.

"Yes! I can't wait to peek into *every* room, but I love the outdoors too and will enjoy a walk about the castle walls." Mina said with an unexpected yawn. She hoped she would awake at dawn to see the pink sky.

"That sounds like fun Mistress Mina! Now, to bed you go. A new day will be fast upon us. May you have pleasant dreams!" Grace twittered while pouring a small pitcher of water into the washbasin.

Mina was so tired, that as she looked warily to the shuttered windows, she half expected to catch a glance of a grassland fairy come to dance on her head.

"To bed! To bed!" Repeated the maid. "You'll need your energy, for I am told you'll have a horse riding lesson tomorrow afternoon as well. Goodnight."

And with that, Grace slipped out of the chamber door and closed it softly behind her. Lomina quickly changed out of her travel clothes, dusty and wrinkled from the journey, and dressed in her sleeping gown. She washed her hands and face in the warm water of the basin and then jumped into bed, soon cozy beneath the covers.

Horse riding lessons! She was surprised her parents hadn't told her of this special treat sooner; how eager Mina was to learn how to ride well. They had been so busy however, with all of the commotion when they'd arrived after dark. She herself had felt startled awake and then jostled about to get out of the wagon, and they'd all been half-asleep and quiet as they trailed through the castle to their rooms. Lomina smiled as she nodded off to sleep. Her last thought was whether or not her sister Cora had been assigned *such* a fine room as hers.

Chapter Five

Mina's eyes fluttered open the next morning as yellow light burst into her room. Grace was humming and bustling through the chamber and had just opened wide the shuttered windows. Lomina sat up in bed, it was to be another beautiful summer day! Only, she was disappointed to have woken so late. Surely it was already far past dawn, for there was no pink hue to be seen. She had a great many dawns and dusks ahead of her however. She would see it for herself and soon. Looking around the room, she felt as well rested as ever and could see a delicious breakfast laid out for her at the hearthside table. The fire had long gone out, but she could still see a few moldering red embers.

Hopping out of bed, she blurted out a gracious 'thank you' to Grace, for she had such an appetite this morning. On the table, there was fresh toasty bread with little clay pots of honey and churned butter to spread upon it. Several kinds of ripe fruit was sliced and displayed on a wooden plate: apple, pear and melon. There was also a hunk of white cheese partially wrapped in thin linen, with a knife before it to cut off a share. There was a cup too, poured high with frothy milk. Lomina sat to the table and began feasting; it was *so* delicious!

"But wait!" She blurted out to Grace mid-bite, a bunch of breadcrumbs stuck to her mouth. "Where are my sister, brother and parents? Am I not to eat with them in the great hall? I saw it last night, it was *so* grand." She'd been so hungry that she'd forgotten all about her family. Back home in their manor house, they'd always eaten together, except when her father was away on king's business.

"They have all eaten in their rooms as you are. And now, Ackerly is at his Latin lesson with his tutor while Cora sits to practice her lute. Your esteemed father is in his meeting chamber with several other local nobles. They are wasting no time discussing what is to be done." Grace informed her as she went about unpacking the rest of Lomina's things.

"Done? About what?" She asked, then taking a big gulp of milk.

"About the unicorns." The handmaiden said matter-of-factly, as if it was hardly news for surprise.

Mina's eyes grew large, her hair messy and tangled with the braids in her hair that she'd not unwound the night before. Around her mouth was a ring of milk, which she quickly wiped away with a soft cloth napkin. "The *unicorns*?"

"Yes." Grace replied with hardly any expression on her face as she worked to hang dresses in the wooden closet. "And your goodly mother is busy with the household, touring the kitchen and pantry, the gardens too, just as any lady overseeing their new home would do. She's ordered roasted carrots and spiced fish pie for the evening meal. How I do love fish pie!" Her expression quickly brightened to relay that night's menu.

"Grace! Spiced fish pie! I want to hear about *the unicorns*!" She threw her hands into the air dramatically and then grabbed for a slice of apple. "I knew they lived in a handful of enchanted forests, but I didn't know that they lived *here*." She took a nibble of crisp apple and then continued speaking while she chewed. "I've never even beheld one. Are they as beautiful as my father has said they are? Are they as magical as the ancient books say?" She was enthralled by this news.

"Ha-ha! I see I've got your attention now, haven't I? Truth is, I have only seen one here and there and from a distance. They sometimes wander out from the Boundless Woods, where they've thrived since ancient days. You can see the forest from your windows. They sometimes gallop out from their woodland and into the fields just below, at dawn or dusk. They forage on the sweet grasses and run as wild horses do, but soon roam back into the forest." Grace explained. "*Yes*, they are beautiful. And yes, people speak of their magic; but that, I haven't seen with my own eyes. It might not be true, for people make up tales. Those animals scare easily and don't get close to people, so I don't know what magic people have seen."

Grace plucked a slice of pear from off of the table and then began folding linens at the closet. "If anyone will learn the truth of it, I'd guess it will be Lord Umberly. They are his first mission while he lodges here, by the king's command. Well aren't these pretty!" The maid said, coming across Mina's collection of colorful hair ribbons in her trunk. "We'll need to comb that hair of yours. Which shall we tie to the end of a new braid?"

Mina pointed to a yellow ribbon and smiled. Her father's first mission! Why hadn't anyone told her this? She always felt like the last to know everything. What exciting news! She was filled with questions.

"But what is the trouble? What is so pressing about the unicorns, for I hear you have some unruly midge dragons here? Aren't *they* more troublesome?" She inquired.

Midge dragons were no larger than a cat with wings. However, they were a terrible nuisance when their populations got out of control. They snatched up chickens and piglets from farms, and would even have tried to carry off a human newborn if it weren't for protective mothers who swatted the pests away from their houses with their brooms. They loved to soar together at night under the light of the moon and caught bats in their fangs to bring back to the fledglings in their nests. Baby midge dragons frenzied over the meat of bats!

But sometimes, a cluster of these reptiles were lured by the bright flames of a festive country bonfire, or the firelight emanating from a great hall (such as the one inside Castle Eerie), believing it was the light of the moon. They'd fly straight into the blaze or in through an open window, causing chaos as they swirled about screeching, causing panic. There was nothing worse than getting a nipping, hissing, shrieking midge dragon caught in your hair, tromping on your dinner plate, or catching its tail on fire to spread to cottage rooftops or flammable furnishings. At the moment, the local lands were said to be overrun by them, causing people to fear going out-of-doors after nightfall, for the dragons were nocturnal.

"That *is* a problem mistress, but according to the king, those little beasts can wait another day. The unicorns however, are in immediate need of help." Grace walked over to the fireplace and poked at the failing embers to help them to burn out completely. "You see, several centuries ago, those glorious horses lived not just in remote woods, or just in a few realms. They ran in herds and were not at all the rare creatures that they are today. There were *many* and they were everywhere that land was found." She reached for a hand broom and began sweeping out the ashes.

"But in the years since that time, huntsmen all the world over have hunted them, without the permission of their kings and rulers, whose responsibility it is to protect *all* the creatures in their realms. What is left of their herds around here have been driven into Boundless Woods. You Lomina, are yet young and so believe that unicorns were always rare, and only lived in mystical forests. But that is not so, for they once were numerous indeed." Grace patiently explained, wiping her ashy hands on her half apron.

"But why do they want to hunt them, Grace? I've never heard of anyone training one to ride as they do with wild horses." Furrowing her brow, she looked completely puzzled.

"You are right. Unicorns are far too wild to ever tame for people's mounts. It is for their horns. They are made of the most lustrous, shimmering, beautifully coiled white bone." The maid began making the bed. "Those horns are magnificent and greatly coveted. They are used to make jewelry, and those pieces are said to be finer than even pure and polished silver and gold. They are crafted into chalices and various decorations, but only for the most greedy, rich and powerful. Some of these wealthy people live here in our own realm, and fuel the unicorns' eternal destruction. Others are from distant lands. This is a problem throughout the world. And what high prices those horns fetch."

"How terrible!" Mina exclaimed. "But how has this diminished the unicorns? How has it driven them into just a few forests?"

"That is a good question. You see, the hunters cannot approach those wild animals peacefully, for a unicorn will always run from a person in fear. A huntsman cannot simply tie up the beast, and cut off the horn leaving the animal alive. No, not even if he wanted to for a unicorn is too feral. Even if they catch them up in great nets, they thrash around, kicking with their strong legs, screaming woefully, hurting themselves and the hunters. There is no way to still them in order to remove their horns and set them free. I know this is too sad to learn mistress, but they shoot them with strong arrows from a distance, some tipped in poison."

Lomina quickly swallowed a bite of bread and then sniffled, wiping her eyes with the back of her hand.

"Are you sure you want to hear this, milady? Or should we start working on a pretty plait for your hair and speak about something kinder?" Grace clucked her tongue, looking concerned.

"Not yet Grace, please do go on. I am my father's daughter and should know these things. I am so glad he has come to help the unicorns." She rose her head up confidently.

The maid sat down on the second seat aside her, cutting off a small bite of cheese and continued on. "And so, the last of these noble creatures have gone into the forests where they can remain better hidden from the eyes of greedy hunters. It is the only safe place for them to raise their young. Once, they ran with their colts and fillies in open fields and even cantered on the sandy seashores. They are far less in number now, whittled away by the hunt, and our king is worried that they will disappear altogether from our lands. He cannot protect all of the world's unicorns, but he *can* do something to save ours. King Olin would never wear a crown made from a unicorn's horn, not for all the wealth in the world. That is why the people love him, because he is good in his heart. Long may he reign."

Lomina was overwhelmed with this news. She'd had no idea of the dire situation that the unicorns were facing. There had been no unicorns near to their previous home and she'd never heard her father speak of something like this before. This was probably because he'd always been assigned wild nuisances that needed some careful solving, such as that cloud of thieving fairies. But this was not some enchanted band causing problems for villagers, but rather human citizens of their *own* realm, making trouble for the enchanted.

Chapter Six

Lomina was sitting proudly upon a pretty white mare with the softest of coats. They were walking with ease behind her new horse master. Her sister, who being a little older was more practiced, carefully trotted on ahead. Someday soon, Mina would be trotting too, even galloping! Riding on a horse was a privilege, for they were not animals just to be mastered, but were strong and intelligent creatures that deserved to be respected. A horse taken well care of would safely carry its rider through many years, over vast lands, and even into fierce battle. One day soon, she would own her own horse and would go out to the stables each day to visit with it and ride. She would speak gently to her horse, and brush it. It would be a girl horse and she would weave beautiful braids into its mane and give it a special name. She'd lead her mare to the plushest patches of green to nibble, and to cool, fresh streams so that she could drink. They would be the best of friends. For all Mina knew, the very horse she rode, would soon belong to her. The horse master had called her Pearl. She thought that was an elegant name.

Cora laughed effervescently, her dark blond hair bouncing inside a blue threaded snood as she rode. Her horse had stubbornly stopped and snorted several times, a rich brown steed with a glossy coat. She guided her mount so that it met with Mina's. Within moments, they were walking side by side. She laughed once more and then pointed something out in the grass, at almost a whisper.

"Do you see any Mina? Thunder was just startled by one in the grass! The reaction he had sounded like a snorting sneeze!" Cora laughed again, her face blushed with the fresh air and her eyes darting over the pasture. "*There* Mina, *look*!"

They'd fallen a little behind the horse master, whose mind seemed on other matters as he continued along on his black steed.

Lomina searched the tall, lush blades of green, squinting as she did so. But the sun was bright and she couldn't see anything but the grass, the colorful faces of wildflowers, and a few random insects flying over them. Dragonflies and honeybees, she presumed.

"I don't see anything Cora. The insects? Is your big, strong Thunder afraid of a bug? Ha-ha!" Mina giggled at her sister.

"You'll see! They visited me last night, and the dreams were so colorful!" Cora smiled.

Lomina gasped, "Fairies! *Where*! No wonder your horse was nervous, don't horses dislike any enchanted creature? Where? Do you still see one?"

"No, but I'm sure we will again. I bet this field is *filled* with them!" Cora said, gently kicking her heels into Thunder's sides.

"Wait! You may have dreamt, but how did you know that they had been there when you woke in the morning? Mother said they'd leave their mark!" She was eager to hear what Cora had experienced.

"Ha-ha!" She laughed as she began to trot off once more, her face prettier than ever in the sunlight. "You'll have to see for yourself, sister. One morning soon, I'm sure!"

And with that, Cora rode away. Mina was now well behind the horse master, and her sister was gaining ground on him. But it was no matter. Today's lesson was getting accustomed to her horse, and walking through the field with the grace of a noble. Mina thought she'd been doing a good job of it so far, and lifted her chin a little higher.

"He-he-heee!" A strange little voice twittered into her ear.

What *was* that? Surely Cora had been teasing her all along. She probably hadn't encountered fairies in this field, they were too elusive. It was also unlikely that they'd twirled on her head last night, Cora always liked to trick her.

Zzzzz...the sound of fast and fluttering wings zipped past her other ear. It sounded like a mosquito that had flown too close to her face, or perhaps it was a cicada passing by. Zzzzz...went the sound once more. And in an instant, there *it* was. A tiny grassland fairy, the most precious thing she'd ever seen. It hovered so close before her face that Mina had to cross her eyes to see it properly. Its wings fluttered so fast, that she could hardly see them at all, just like a hummingbird's! It was a girl fairy, wearing bits of grass that were woven into an emerald colored dress. Atop a head full of long dark hair, tangled as ever, sat a head wreath weaved with the tiniest parts of flowers. How delicate and magical a grassland fairy was!

For a moment, Mina forgot the usual fears,

about one pinching her or casting some short-lived spell. She could spend an entire day observing these little beings, and would one day take a picnic far out in the field and do just that! Well, maybe when she was a little braver perhaps.

Just then, the little creature zipped off and in her place, a boy fairy whizzed in to flutter afore her. Only, instead of just before her nose, it flitted before Pearl's face. The horse instantly stopped in its tracks and whinnied. Agitated, she began to raise up one of her knees, only to clomp down her hoof, soon repeating this with her other leg. She cried out a second time, more loudly and then snorted through her nose as the boy fairy hovered close-by.

Mina began to feel nervous as Pearl continued to prance. She grasped at the reins more tightly while trying to speak gently to the mare. It was difficult to make out the fairy's exact expression, but it appeared as though the horse had entranced the mite; what a monster such a mare would look like to a fairy!

Pearl continued to prance in place and though Lomina's gentle words placated the horse somewhat, fear was still evident in her glossy black eyes. It was a wonder how easily startled horses could become in but an instant. Mina tried to shoo the fairy away, but it continued to flit before the animal. And then, the mischievous little being did something to set the horse into a fit. Landing on top of the mare's head, it began to hop around in a wild dance! Lomina could not believe her eyes! Was the fairy boy trying to give Pearl enchanted daydreams, much like the pleasant dreams they gave to people whose heads they danced upon in the night? Or, was he such a naughty creature that he was purposefully trying to upset her horse? She had a mind to brush the fairy away with a gentle swipe of her hand, but it was too late.

Pearl reared back out of fear from the fairy boy's lively jig and began to swing its head wildly. The fairy flew off and away, as fast as could be, but the horse remained as upset as ever. The mare started into a gallop and Mina let out a single sharp screech. Within seconds, she'd passed up both her sister and the riding master. She'd have continued to scream out with fear, only she needed to concentrate; as they flew over the field, she knew that her situation was serious. If she didn't hold on for dear life, she would be flung from the horse as the fairy had been, only she didn't have wings to keep her from falling hard to the ground. She could be terribly injured.

A deep sob ran up into her throat and her eyes were filled with the look of terror. If only there was a way to stop the horse, she would scurry off and *never* ride again! But there was no stopping Pearl, who dashed through the pasture at lightening speed. Tall grasses whipped at Mina's slippered feet, in their place within their stirrups and squeezing forcefully into the horse's sides. Tears began to fall down her face and her braid loosened, wisps of hair were flying into her eyes.

Mina could hear her sister screeching, as well as the horseman's boisterous yells, but they were far behind her and growing more distant still. Was Pearl running so fast that the horse master couldn't catch up to them? It seemed so. If only he could drive his horse up beside hers and calm this wild mare to a halt. She was too unsteady on her saddle to look behind her and see how close he was.

In no time, they were approaching the Boundless Woods, crossing over from the field through bushes and bramble. They were heading right into the enchanted forest! With as terrified as Pearl had been of the fairy, this woodland was the worst possible place for her to go. Mina cried out breathlessly for the horse to stop, but the animal would not heed her and they were soon riding beneath a canopy of ancient, leafy boughs. Even with the rougher terrain, still the horse would not stop. She bounded over fallen logs, ran past stinging branches and careened around mossy boulders. To see this horse and rider, anyone would have claimed that Mina was the most courageous of equestrians.

Through her tears and stark fear, she continued to hold tightly to the reins, and to watch the path so that she could do her very best to move with the animal as it veered this way and that. It took all of Lomina's bravery to keep her wits about her. At that moment, she'd have rather faced a fire-breathing dragon than to have been on that ride, as long as her feet could touch the ground.

Once more, she pleaded with the beast. The animal was not galloping as fast as in the field because of the rugged forest floor, but was still yet running. Mina could tell that the horse was getting tired however, for it was breathing heavily. She also, was becoming greatly fatigued and didn't know how much longer she could hold on.

"Pearl...*please*. Slow, *slow down* gentle mare! Whoa there...*whoa*." She breathlessly uttered as kindly as she was able.

In that moment, the horse *finally* heard her plea and gradually cooled out of its run, soon walking though the woods. Mina was in a daze and desperately wanted to get down, but she feared any sudden moves would startle the horse once more. Both worked to catch their breaths as they ambled onwards for a time, deeper into the forest. Finally, Pearl came to a stop just before a bubbling, glittering creek.

Chapter Seven

After consoling the creature (even though she could have used the consoling herself), Mina felt comfortable enough to dismount from the horse. Though the animal had taken her on the most dangerous race of her life, she knew deep down that Pearl had only been acting naturally and hadn't meant to frighten her. It had been an upsetting flight for them both.

Walking slowly, she gently led Pearl by the reins to a young tree and slackly tied her to it so that the horse could nibble on the patchy grass at the bottom of the trunk. Looking around them, she knew that they were deep in the forest. They had changed directions frequently and they were now lost. She knotted the rein, not chancing that Pearl would startle and run away, leaving her all alone.

Scanning the wild wood, it looked to her like any other, thick with green and birdsong.

She'd have been able to admire it better if she'd not been told of how mystical and strange the Boundless Woods were. She might have even tried to lead the horse back by its rein on foot, if she wasn't afraid of what magical creatures they might meet. It didn't matter anyway, for she didn't know which direction would point them back to the castle or deeper into the woods. They weren't going anywhere.

Taking account of herself, she found that her hair had come completely loose of the intricate plait that Grace had weaved into it that morning, and that her favored yellow hair ribbon was gone. It had surely flitted away right out of her braid during her heroic flight. Mina's pretty embroidered slippers and the fine fabric of her gown, were ripped in places and striped with green and brown where grass and branches had left their mark. Her elbow-length dress sleeves were also in tatters, and the skin on the bare parts of her arms were scratched and beginning to sting. But in spite of all of this, Mina still knew how fortunate she had been. A missing ribbon, a torn gown and a few scratches; these were nothing compared to if she'd been thrown from the horse riding full speed.

Ambling up to the fresh, trickling stream, Lomina bent low and washed her hands in the water, soon splashing it over her face and arms. The cool water felt nice, for she was overly warm; not only had the ride been exhausting, but the day was hot. She swatted away a mosquito that had begun annoyingly buzzing around her ear and then reviewed her reflection in the stream.

Though her image in the water was blurry, she could still tell that she looked a fright. Mina laughed, she felt like a scarecrow! Leaning closer to the water, she took up a scoop and brought it to her lips. It was cold and refreshing. But just then, she was startled to see in the reflection that she was not alone. Pearl was there in the image too, standing just beside her! Perhaps she'd tied the knot of the rein too loosely. It was only natural that the parched horse would also want to get a drink as well, for if Lomina thirsted, the horse would be even thirstier! But as the animal's head bent down toward the running water, she immediately noticed something peculiar. Was that a twisted *horn*?

Mina whipped her head around to look at the horse but could not believe her eyes. It was not Pearl at all, whom she could see from the corner of her eye was still tied securely to the tree. The animal beside her was a *unicorn*!

Lomina was absolutely amazed to see one of these majestic creatures. Though it looked not unlike her own horse, at the top of its head sprouted a spiraled horn, looking as magical and precious as a regal crown. The unicorn also had intelligent eyes, as though this breed of animal was far wiser than the most well-trained, cleverest of steeds. After it took a sip of water, they both momentarily looked into each other's faces, and then the unicorn drank once more. When Mina had looked into its eyes, she felt certain that there *was* magic behind them, but what powers the unicorn could perform, she might never know.

The encounter was over in an instant, for in a sudden flash, the unicorn lifted its proud and lovely horn, the twisted bone shining like polished marble, and sniffed the air. In seconds, the unicorn bounded past her and over the narrow waterway, galloping away into the woods as a flash of white. But what had frightened it away? Surely the creature hadn't been afraid of she and Pearl? Mina couldn't believe how close the animal had come to her, leaning over the water right next to her to partake in her respite. She hadn't startled it, and there certainly didn't seem to be any pesky grassland fairies about. Was there something *else* lurking nearby?

Just as the last remnant of white from the fleeing unicorn disappeared out of sight, Mina stood tall, and an arrow zipped right past her! It hit the very sapling that Pearl was tied up to with a deadly thwack. She instantly shuddered over how close it had come to them, as the horse stirred in surprise. So *that* was it, there was a huntsman in their midst! Lomina turned her head to look behind her and easily spied the man at a distance. He was working to fix a fresh arrow into his longbow. Lifting the weapon once more, he pointed it directly at Pearl. Mina's heart instantly began to race for she knew that she only had a second to save her horse. She was sure that the huntsman thought the mare was the very unicorn that had just run through. Sucking in a deep breath, her body trembling, she yelled out to the man. With great courage in the midst of a dangerous hunter, she bellowed.

"By the order of King Olin, put down your bow!" She was startled by the power in her own voice as she nervously waited for his reaction.

The huntsman slowly took his aim from Pearl and safely pointed the arrow back toward the ground, letting go of the grip until the weapon was slack. As he looked at Mina, he seemed momentarily baffled. There was a confused look on his face, which made it clear that he'd never seen Lomina near the stream just yards from her horse. His sights had been on the large white animal, and he had seen nothing else. He looked back to Pearl, and she could see that he realized his mistake. This was no unicorn.

The leather-clad huntsman, camouflaged in his garb of brown and green, his brown hair messy and his face unshaven, began laughing into the air. He yelled back to Mina.

"Ha-ha! This will teach you to ride your horse into the Boundless Woods, young mistress! With a white mare at that! You narrowly saved your horse's life, for I thought it was quite another creature of this forest. Now, be off! Explore no more in these woods, unless you care not for your life!"

The woodsman began to march off, but Mina couldn't help but to call out once more. She knew that the man would continue his search for a unicorn and she had to do *something*.

"By the king's command I say! For you are poaching and it is against the law of this realm to harm a unicorn!" She yelled out toward his back. Her body was truly trembling now, for she was not used to making commands of a stranger, or anyone at all. Especially for she was yet young, and he, a dangerous looking man.

The huntsman swiveled around mid-stride

and rebuked her, "And *what*, pray tell me, will *you* do about it? Get thee home!"

Though she knew that it was imprudent, and that this man seen hunting a unicorn might lash out at her with his temper, she mustered the last of her courage to change his course. "*I* can do nothing sir. But my father is Toly Umberly, in service of the king, and he is in these woods even now. He has armed men in his midst, a band of loyal subjects looking for poachers like *you*!"

She'd told a lie, for who knew whether her father was in the woods or not. And if he were, he was certainly on the lookout for his missing daughter, not a poacher. However, her words carried weight, for the man paused a moment while holding a quizzical look.

"Lord Umberly, you say? The king's wrangler of enchanted beings? Slayer of dragons?" He spurted.

Mina knew that her father was no slayer of

beasts, for he was a peaceful man. However, if he had a frightful reputation, now was the time to use it to her advantage.

"The very one, huntsman! Wait, I hear them now!" She yelled, forcing a proud smile on her face. There was in fact rustling of leaves and branches coming from just behind a nearby thicket. Had they found her so soon?

The huntsman heard it too, and sprinted out in the opposite direction. He looked like a frightened deer, or a horse running away from a grassland fairy! Her plan had worked! As she watched him scamper away, she knew that he would take no unicorn's life; at least not today.

Chapter Eight

The rustling in the bushes was getting louder and Pearl was visibly growing uneasy, rearing her head and neighing anxiously. Mina was growing nervous as well, for if it had been the horse master or any of the men from the castle, she'd have heard them call out to her. They certainly wouldn't be hiding in the bushes!

What was here? She could only imagine with it being an enchanted wood. It might be a mighty troll with stinky breath, come out to play his tricks. Or perhaps it was a grouchy cave dragon looking for his next meal. Or maybe it was not a creature of the enchanted world at all. It might be a ferocious and clawed bear or a shaggy, sharp-toothed wolf. Mina shivered to imagine it. Oh, how she wanted to escape these woods! Must she be courageous yet again? How much bravery could one girl muster in one day?

"Who goes there? Please show yourself, for you are frightening my horse." Lomina blurted with what force she had left, out towards the thick greenery, with its noisy, shaking leaves.

The tension was getting to the point that she felt like she would faint and she gasped as briar entwined with ivy and green leafy branches parted way, fluidly as if by some unnatural command. And out of it, stepped an elegantly tall woman with long ebony hair. She wore a shimmering cream-colored gown with sleeves so long, that they fell past her sides. Upon her head rested a glorious wreath weaved from ivy. Her skin was luminous and her eyes sparkled with both strength and kindness. She strangely lacked Mina's rumpled clothing, and appeared perfectly cool for such a warm summer day. This was very odd to be seen on *anyone* traipsing through a wild wood. Was this woman lost, just as she was? Just then, the woman spoke.

"Good day, mistress. Have you found yourself adrift from your way?" The woman's voice sounded like music. She began walking in Mina's direction and did it so gracefully, that she appeared to be floating. This was definitely one of the most refined noblewomen Lomina had ever met. She could have even passed for a queen.

"Why yes, I have. Are you lost too madam?" Mina tried to smile, but felt shabby and awkward. She was also tired and hungry, but perhaps this woman would know the way back to the castle.

The stranger laughed pleasantly, "Why no, I am not lost. For I live here, in these woods."

Mina gasped, "*Oh*. I didn't know that *any* people lived in this forest, for they say that it is a magical place, where only woodland animals, enchanted creatures and wild beasts live."

The charming woman smiled and her face

radiated grace. "But you are right, dear girl! However, I am *not* a person. I am an elf."

Lomina's mouth went agape and she was lost for words. An elf! That would explain why she looked so, so *perfect*! She had sometimes heard noble ladies, and handmaidens too, gossip over elfish beauty. They'd wonder over female elves' alluring secrets, though everyone knew that their loveliness didn't come from face colors and tonics. They were simply born with enchanting looks.

Mina was speechless. As pretty as this being was, and as much as she glowed with the aura of goodness, elves *were* magical and she needed to remain wary. However, at that moment, her mother's words came to mind. She'd been reminded to act kindly toward any enchanted creature she might meet, excepting dragons and ogres.

"It is a pleasure to meet you. I have never before met an elf. I was told that elf women were very handsome, and it is true! I am Lomina, and I abide in Castle Eerie. My family and I have just arrived, just last night in fact. This afternoon, my horse Pearl ran off from a riding lesson, and I with her! A grassland fairy made her wild by dancing on her head. She *did not* like that." She shared.

The elf laughed delightedly. "I see! Those fairies *do* love to frolic. But poor white mare...she'll soon recover from her fright. I am glad to see too, that her free run left you quite unharmed. Someday soon, you'll look back on it as a great adventure."

"Thank you. I hope I do, though at present, I am certainly eager to get home again." Mina confided.

"Yes, I can understand. Soon you will be on your way there, but first, I have a gift for you." The elf woman said, coming closer.

A gift? Mina was leery. Why would this elf give *her* a gift?

"Do not be afraid. Quite simply, I was witness to your selfless deed. You were very brave in trying to send that huntsman off, and clever too, though it could have proved dangerous; and all to save a unicorn. What a special heart and a great courage you have." Lauded the elf.

Mina shook her head with disbelief; this day certainly *couldn't* get any stranger. But would it?

"Your valor deserves to be recognized. And so, I am gifting you with *one* wish." She was now standing just a few feet away. "When dusk comes, and the sky becomes a rosy hue on this day, look to the brightest star in the sky and make a wish. However, be careful, for a wish is powerful. Ask only for something that you truly desire. It shall be yours."

"Thank you! But...I do not deserve such a mighty gift!" Mina uttered, disbelieving.

With her last word, the echoes of horse

hooves and the clamor of men's voices could be heard in the distance and she looked away. Her name was being called out into the forest, and she knew that she would soon be delivered to safety and back to the castle. Looking back to the enchanted woman, there was no one there. She had disappeared.

Chapter Nine

As she sat upon the back of her father's steed, with his carefully riding them home, Mina took great care to think over what she would wish for. She already had everything a girl could ever want: good health, family, happiness, excellent fare and nice clothes. So what would be the best wish to make?

Looking back toward that daring mare Pearl, who followed behind the men's horses, trotting merrily toward home, Mina smiled and thought she knew.

And so, once upon a star in the glowing pink of dusk, as the sun fell slowly behind the horizon and the stars came out to twinkle, a wish was made. Amidst the waking midge dragons squalling from the trees and the grassland fairies hurrying toward their cozy nests, Lomina spoke the words. *I wish that the horns of unicorns will forever be hidden from the eyes of men.*

And so it was. Upon the brightest star, by the magic granted by one gracious elf in those wild and unpredictable Boundless Woods, the horn of every unicorn disappeared from human sight. Forever after, those creatures flourished and roamed without fear, extending far out from the forests, for no one was the wiser that they were actually unicorns rather than horses. They were safely disguised from every hunter's arrow.

Most people believed that these creatures had all died out, that they'd been hunted down to the last unicorn and were gone forever. Even Toly Umberly was grieved to explain to the king that he'd not made it to Castle Eerie in time. But King Olin knew that it was not his fault; it had been a dire problem for some time already, and he should have addressed it sooner. Throughout all the realms, unicorns had seemingly disappeared. *Everyone* had been too late to save them.

Lomina never told anyone of her wish, and kept the unicorns' secret for all of her life. But every now and then, she met a wild horse with eyes so intelligent that she smiled, for she was in the midst of a unicorn.

Before bed, on the very night that Lomina had made such a kind wish from her heart, Grace carefully combed out all of the thorny forest burs and tangles from her hair, until her tresses were soft and shiny. How easily (after such an incredible day) did Lomina fall fast asleep in her bed. As she slept, she had the most glorious, happy dreams, all the nightlong. When she woke the next morning, she was surprised to see her reflection. Wild tangles, bits of nature and one pretty yellow ribbon tied haphazardly into her hair. So *this* was the surprise that grassland fairies left behind after dancing on one's head to stir up pleasant dreams! Mina liked her new hairstyle, and would wear it proudly this day as she went to explore all of the other mysteries that Castle Eerie had yet in store for her!

Once Upon A Star

60660712R00052

Made in the USA
Middletown, DE
15 August 2019